T0199022

CAN'T NEVER COULD!

by

Pat Sabiston

www.patsabistonauthor.com

Illustrations by Taylor Johnson

Instagram: @taylorjohnsonart

WestBow Press books may be ordered through booksellers or by contacting:

WestBow Press
A Division of Thomas Nelson & Zondervan
1663 Liberty Drive
Bloomington, IN 47403
www.westbowpress.com
844-714-3454

Because of the dynamic nature of the Internet, any web addresses or links contained in this book may have changed since publication and may no longer be valid. The views expressed in this work are solely those of the author and do not necessarily reflect the views of the publisher, and the publisher hereby disclaims any responsibility for them.

Interior Image Credit: Taylor Johnson

Scriptures taken from the Holy Bible, New International Version®, NIV®. Copyright © 1973, 1978, 1984, 2011 by Biblica, Inc.™ Used by permission of Zondervan. All rights reserved worldwide. www.zondervan.com The "NIV" and "New International Version" are trademarks registered in the United States Patent and Trademark Office by Biblica, Inc.®

ISBN: 978-1-6642-0729-5 (sc)
ISBN: 978-1-6642-0728-8 (hc)
ISBN: 978-1-6642-0730-1 (e)

Library of Congress Control Number: 2020918928

Print information available on the last page.

WestBow Press rev. date: 10/14/2020

This book is DEDICATED TO

Our Children … Grandchildren … and Great Grands!

Daughters *Adrienne* and *Laura* who never lost their love of *The Secret Garden*; and who gave

us the most wonderful grandsons in the world … *Trey* and *Hunter*!

Daughter *Kristie* who trusted me to care for her precious daughter, *Brandi* … our Grand Girl …

who was the inspiration for this book.

and
for
Peyton and *Emma*
(Our GREAT Grands!)

Girls, may you grow into being the courageous women

who came before you.

Boys, never forget your rich history … that you were "made of better stock."

STAND!

Brandi and her mother lived in a little town, in a tiny house, just big enough for the two of them.

They were *never* separated, until one day …

1

Mommy told Brandi she had to travel on business, so Brandi would stay with her grandmother. Brandi didn't know this woman, because she lived far away.

Mommy would be gone only four days, and Brandi could count down the days on her fingers. Mommy told Brandi her grandmother had already raised two girls, so she'd be fun to be around.

When they arrived, Grams – as she was called – gave Brandi a big smile and an enormous hug. Brandi felt right at home. Mommy waved goodbye, and the adventure began.

Grams took Brandi shopping, where she was allowed to pick out *all* her favorite food.

6

At dinner, Brandi stared at the buttery corn on the cob.

"Grams, I want this so much, but I really don't think I can eat it without my two front teeth."

CAN'T NEVER COULD!

"You'll find a way because can't never could," said Grams with a smile. Brandi picked up the corn and began chewing it with the teeth on the side of her mouth, enjoying every bite!

When Brandi took her bath, she was sad there were no bath toys until Grams gave her a shiny bowl from the kitchen and rotary beaters that made huge mounds of suds for play.

"When you use your imagination, things become more fun," said Grams.

At bedtime, Grams read a story about a little girl and a secret garden and promised an adventure the next day.

But Brandi couldn't fall asleep in the strange, dark bedroom.

So, Grams sat beside her and told her a story of how God gave a little boy courage so that he could slay a mean giant with only a rock and slingshot.

Grams' voice was soothing as more stories flowed, so Brandi didn't even remember falling asleep.

After breakfast, Grams and Brandi put on matching garden gloves and tromped into the yard. They dug and planted, and planted and dug. Then, Grams placed a rock, with writing on it, in the middle of the plants.

"Can you read what it says?" asked Grams.

Brandi sounded out the words: "O-u-r Se-cret Gar-den."

"Correct!" exclaimed Grams. "Now, this will be our special spot to remember as we make more memories."

In the afternoon, Grams and Brandi put on their skates, but Brandi saw sweet gum balls all over the sidewalk.

"Oh, noooo, Grams! We can't skate now, because these are in the way!" Brandi pouted.

"Can't never could, Little Miss," said Grams as she grabbed a broom from the garage and swept away the pods. Then, off they went like a flash!

The next day, it was raining. Grams made a fort of sheets over a table, and Brandi played make-believe all day under the cozy covers. Then, Grams showed her how to make a castle out of boxes, glue, and construction paper.

"Imagination is fun!" Brandi squealed with delight.

The next day dawned sunny and bright. Grams suggested Brandi try to ride her bicycle *without* the training wheels.

"Oh, I couldn't," sighed Brandi.

"Remember what I've taught you." Grams repeated the words slowly. "Can't – never – could!"

Grams held on to the back of the bicycle seat and ran behind Brandi until she got her balance. Before long, Brandi was pedaling all by herself and was so proud!

On their last day together, Grams and Brandi watched old movies that were only in black and white. The one Brandi liked the most was of a little girl who sang and danced.

Soon, Brandi learned one of the songs by heart … *"On the Good Ship Lollipop,"* … and Grams told her she could perform it for her mother.

Brandi said, "Oh, but I can't sing very well."

"Now, what have I taught you?" Grams asked.

"Can't never could!" said Brandi with a big grin.

So, Brandi began to sing and, using her imagination, made up fun dance steps.

While Grams was fixing dinner, Brandi asked to borrow some scissors. Grams was busy preparing the food and wasn't really paying attention to Brandi.

Once again, Brandi wanted to use her imagination by cutting off one of her long dresses to look just like the little girl in the movies they had watched.

But right before Brandi could cut into the fabric, Grams ran into the room and yelled, "S-T-O-P!"

Brandi's eyes grew wide with fear, but Grams gave her a huge bear hug.

"One last lesson," said Grams. "Just because you *can* do something doesn't always mean you *should*!"

When Mommy arrived, Brandi told her all about skating, even though the path seemed blocked … and how she played make-believe using her imagination.

But Brandi was most excited about trying new things, even when she was afraid.

"Like this!" screamed Brandi, hopping on her bike and racing around the driveway.

On their last day, Brandi gave Grams a goodbye hug and kiss as her mother began packing the automobile.

"I don't think all this stuff is going to fit inside this little car," said Mommy. At the very same time, Grams and Brandi yelled:

"CAN'T NEVER COULD!"

As Brandi and her mother drove away, Brandi knew she and her Grams would make many more memories in the future.

But more important, Brandi knew, *for sure*, she would never again say, "I can't."

Internal Content Scriptures
- When you are lonely and scared (Isaiah 41:10)
- When you are discouraged (1 Corinthians 9:24)
- When you can't sleep (Psalms 63:6)
- When you need to decide between right and wrong (1 Timothy 4:12)
- The best advice for parents and grandparents (Proverbs 22:6)

Kids who have healthy self-esteem tend to: feel valued and accepted
- Feel confident that they can do what's expected
- Feel proud of a job well done
- Think good things about themselves
- Feel prepared for everyday challenges

(SOURCE: *Kids' Health* from Nemours)

For Reader/Teacher Discussion:
Help children --
- Realize single-parent families are not unusual
- Understand families don't always live near one another
- Practice counting
- Learn to identify things in nature
- Discuss their favorite foods and what constitutes proper nutrition
- Know being scared of new situations is normal
- Discover how to make memories
- Learn to solve problems.
- Encourage imagination and pure fun
- Know they *can* do anything they set their minds to do
- Use discernment in decision making
- Stay positive, regardless of the obstacles
- Increase self-esteem through accomplishments

Young Readers: ***Is there a story you'd like to share with the author about doing something you didn't think you could?***

www.patsabistonauthor.com

Printed in the United States
By Bookmasters